HOLY
DOORS

HAT & BEARD EDITIONS

HOLY DOORS

POEMS
MANDY KAHN

Holy Doors by Mandy Kahn

First North American Edition, 2023

Copyright © 2023 by Mandy Kahn

Library of Congress Cataloging-in-Publication Data

Names: Kahn, Mandy, author

Title: Holy Doors / Mandy Kahn

Identifiers: ISBN: 978-1-955125-21-5 (hardcover)

Subject: BISAC: Poetry / American / General.

Cover art and design: Robbie Simon

Interior book design: Sabrina Che

ISBN: 978-1-955125-21-5

www.hatandbeard.com

IG: @hatandbeardpress

Hat & Beard Editions books are published by:

Hat & Beard, LLC

713 N. La Fayette Park Place

Los Angeles, CA 90026

HAT & BEARD EDITIONS | LOS ANGELES

For my parents,
Judy Berg
and Arnold Kahn

"Holiness is not a luxury for the few;
it is not just for some people.
It is meant for you and for me
and for all of us."
—Mother Teresa

Everywhere, everywhere,
doors to the holy—

yes, in the silences—

also
in bells—

CONTENTS

THE EVERYDAY

Old friends, old loves, I celebrate
the day-to-day you've found: the favored cup,
the dog, the child, the husband, wife—

the hat rack by the door, the bowl of keys,
the chair in sun,
weekends with your omelets made
just right.

You graduated into
the encyclopedic pleasures of the everyday,
that brighter vision—

the sharp phantasmagoria you enter
when you watch your child through sprinkler water:
that moving prism.

Didn't I always tell you, lover, roommate,
there were portals by the dishtowels?

           You think you left your dreams.

You've entered
the Basilica of the Present
by its common causeway.

           This, your striving earned.

HOLY WORK

I believe we each deserve a prize
for showing up
to be alive.

To start, I will award myself
for walking to the market,
and walking back three blocks
with loaded arms,

for stems I trimmed, the lilies

in a jar I saved and washed and dried
and stored. Here's a prize

for managing my teeth,
restoring order to my hair.

Here's a prize for heating up the soup,
and one for washing out the pan.

We do the work of what we can,

we take a breath and wade across the day.

Every moment must be managed through

by particles of light
in suits of tar and gravel.

Holy work
is all we do.

I DO NOT FEAR DEATH, YET GO ON LIVING

I do not fear death, yet go on living.
I know choirs wait for me to finish,
wait to paint this clear air with their singing,
wait in gauzy figures, just past seeing.
I know what will greet me is more vibrant
than a field of poppies in the morning
widening their petals for the daylight.
I know what is waiting, past my seeing.
Know its luster. Still, I go on living,
chopping, boiling, eating, scrubbing, sweeping,
writing sonnets seen by just my ceiling,
stacking up old bills—paying, not paying,
then a bath, a walk, and it is evening.
Choirs wait to stir the air with feeling.
Angels wait to steer me towards a drawbridge
made of lighted crystal. I keep living.

RAINBOW LINE

Not an arc
above a misty glade,

not between
two cliffs,

not through
waterfall—

    but here,
on this peeling
bathroom wall,

one solid
rainbow line,

straight
as new lead pipe.

From the manmade
shower door,

sharp
as the tools
that cut glass,

not a human finger
but an even strip,

a ruler's edge
of God.

As if he's saying,
I'll use any door.

Yes, I am apparent
in the wet glens,
curving
over daffodils,
decorating streams—

also
on the workbench
with exposed bolts,

also in the foundry,

also on the wrench.

Any glass you've made
and cut

can show me. Any light
contains me. Any wall
might host.

Manufacture, slice—

a prism

finds you. Even sand,
with heat, is glass. I love

every room.

POEM ABOUT THE MOMENT OF DEATH

I won't pretend
I do not know
what happens
the moment we die.

We're flung out
of all worry
the way flower seeds
are launched from their pods.

We'd watch them swell,
those pods, each spring,
in common grass,
when we were young,

trying to implore them
to fling
while we looked.

A flurry of colorless orbs
would burst
from our small scene,

and make their huge arcs,

not while we were waiting,
but after,
when we were deep in

acting out
how we might spend this life.

Then we'd hear
the softest sound,
and a hundred
shell-white spheres
would launch
from our sphere,

past
where we could see.

How those—
uncolored, rough
and slight—
made flowers,

or how they knew
to wait
till we had turned away—

we did not
understand it.

We knew it as
enchantment.

I won't pretend
that I don't know

how death arrives,
seeming to be colorless.

Or how it waits
for us to leave the bedside,
after days,

to stretch our legs, at last,
or to make tea.

I won't pretend
I do not know
the fuchsia fields
its clear arc builds.

A flash
when someone's back is turned,
then

lightness,
flying,
worlds.

MULCH

I might have had concerns
about signing the contract,
and wanted
my lawyer to read it,
with his coffee in one hand,
his wily red pen in the next.

But what's the use?
Things
as we know them
are ending,
new things are starting—

lawyers and judges
will soon be stooped
in their gardens,
learning to grow.

Look at them
in their clogs
and their aprons,
holding up
their spades—
curiosity, passion—
high from the waft
of the soil.

Look at me,

signing
what I have been given,
in my bedhead and bathrobe;

soon
I'll make mulch
and the language it's made with
will show its strange phrases
no more.

THIS DAY

This is one
I thought I'd never write,

about the night
I thought I'd die.

      The ambulance
      came quickly.

            Two firemen
            rolled a gurney.

The wild pain
in my gut
was its own
kind of journey.

The ambulance was moving,
I was inside it,
night scrolled through
dark windows,

      it seemed that I might die.

          And I felt ready.

Had I been given a choice,
I would have stayed here—

written ten more volumes,

first
the one you're holding.

There was
no choosing.

I told Boris—
he was there—
to tell you

all had been forgiven.
I grasped at nothing.

My final thoughts
were loving,

grateful for the things
that I had finished.
They both felt easy—

to stay
like a bird on a branch,

perching, trilling,

with all flight
held within it,

or to go
flying.

Yes, I would have chosen
you, and living.

Even knowing
heaven.

      This day
      was given.

SOME DAYS

Some days I wish to leave my beak
and only be my wings.

No eating, no thought of wormly bodies,
or where they slide,

no crowing, or knowing what's worth crowing,
or when to crow,

no pecking at the hard ground,
or soft ground, for what is there,

or could be, or should be,
or will be,

just flat on air

and turning, like a clock's slim hour hand,
that slow and right.

Warm gust gliding upward,
cool gust gliding down,

me the raft between them,
vast and held aloft—

silent—and full from moving forces—
white static's heir—

not the wind, and not the thing that drives it:
the thing it moves.

A LONGSHOT IN SPRING

This one's for my stepdad, Norm,
who started me betting
the longshots in spring.

We dressed for the races, back then—
I wore curls
and a skirt with lace edging,

and black shoes that buckled
and clacked,

and sometimes
pink tights
and a hat.

I loved betting longshots—

was happy
with losing some contests,

then my twenty-to-one
would come in,

and I'd spread out my winnings,
stacking and fanning my loot,

unfolding the dog-ears
and flattening creases

until I knew each bill by touch.

I loved betting longshots
in spring.

I'd stand
at the teller,

age six,

and collect what I'd earned.

My sisters thought
it was luck. There's more:

I wasn't too timid to lose.

    I'm still not.

Look at this odd longshot
of a life—

    I live
    in perpetual spring.

My hair is straight,
uncombed,
just like a girl's hair,
though I am grown,

and still I have
a girl's clear-sightedness,
unwavering will.

The years
haven't broken me—
a thoroughbred bought
by a farm—

they've
preserved me, like an ether,
an oil.

Girlhood
stilled
in its dreaming,
its faith.

What am I betting on now?
World peace.

Let them guffaw
in the stands.

Let all the chattering jockeys
make jest in the stables.

It's May
in my rooms.

Call it a thousand to one
if you want,
my dream
that we will choose
to live from love,

that I will live
to see that choice.

Here's what I've learned:

sometimes your spring horse comes in,
whom no one else bet on,

your Fire in the Moonlight,

       your Faery's Call,
       your Tall Auspicious Lady,
       your Cherries in Dew.

Look at that child,
counting and folding
the bills they said
had come from luck.

Not luck, or God, or patience. No.

Belief.

THE GEYSER

When we leave our bodies,
either in sleep,
or because we have finished
this life,

       we float
       in form
       without mass.

We float, and hover, and glide,
something like light,

and if we meet another
out of body
if we choose
we can combine.

          I
          have done this
          in dream.

Two beings meet,

and when they lean
to embrace,

instead
they overlap,

and in
their single chest,
a geyser plumes.

The closeness
we accomplish
in the body
is a seeking of that—

where two chests
overlap,

a geyser
of the presence
of one.

> To welcome in
> that wellspring
> we must let our
> edges go.

Soft
we must become,

and
permissible,
permitting.

Then we,
a one

and a one,
permeable,
wide,

hover
in proximity,

eye-locked
and alive,

    and combine.

        I
        have done this
        in dream.

            There's a geyser
            of honeysuckle scent
            in the one chest
            these two share.

As children,
we'd pull
honeysuckle blooms
soft
from the vine,

and suck the backs
to tease out

a fraction of a drop
of golden nectar,
    and hold it on the tongue.

        A geyser
        of that nectar,
        its yellow taste,
        its scent.

When we let
our thinking go

we soften
into what we know.

        Then
        there's only
        vivid
        flow.

WHAT WE'RE DOING

We are in the long breath of creation
blowing into function our own being,
out of that one mouth and into seeing;
all we do is wafted into doing.
Why do we think labor is not loving?
All that seems to strain
is plied with meaning; all that we are given
causes growing. All that seems to stop
is still that flowing. We, together, one,
blow into body:
make ourselves again, and call it living.

MY HEART HAS ROOMS

Unlovable, unloving—
bring them here.
I will love them first.
    My heart
    has rooms.

Years ago, its chambers
had to spread—
soon they'd fit
an apple, a notebook,
a phonebook, a chair.
Soon each was a sitting room,
a chapel, then
a synagogue, then
a Hall of State.
Soon there was the space
for all constituents.
Soon long benches spread.
Soon high doors were spread.

Anyone can love
the young, the old.
Send the hard, the strong—
those whose chambers seem to house
just blood—

        those who were not loved,
        and do not love.

I've built benches
where we'll sit
till heaven
fuses us forever
with plain light, each other.

The hurtful. The brutal.
The cursing. The cold.

By a window under cloud
I'll sit with them,
gingerly, unspeaking,

       until the morning
       we learn why.

GRANDMOTHER AND I

We two—grandmother and I—were masterful
at nothing.

We'd amble
to the rummage store, where old books
cost a dime,

then read away the afternoon,
and watch the high sun cross her carpeting.

I'd move couch to floor, then floor to bed,
and nap, and read, and nap, and read again
on couch or porch or floor. In a wicker chair nearby
she'd read.

No one to observe and note
the better things not done, we sat
in sun, and time made sundials out of us.

One old, one young,
we Connoisseurs of Calm,
we Captains of the Skiff
that Loves its Docking, we experts in
High Rest—no one lounged
like we did. No one saw
the nothing we did well.

ALL YOU HAVE TO DO

What happens is, you survive,
and then,
the next moment.

Impossible, it seems,
to careen
to the future

without finishing tasks
from the present,

but it happens,
a new hour,

and you're there.

And soon
a time arrives
with altered bylaws.

Look:

chairs float
here,

you can ride them,

and there are no banks.

The knots
that had tangled your hairdo
cradle a gosling,

which takes to the air—

downtown
you see choirs
roaming the alleys,

and ballplayers
knit.

Someone hands out
pineapple
on skewers,

and someone
paints flags,

a message arrives on letterhead
saying
You're free now,

and cars run on thought.

Wait. Survive this.
The old rules
die faster
than you do.

Breathe
as the ship of the new way
sails into focus,

blowing its
festival horns.

I VISIT YOU IN ASHLAND

    Instead of writing about peace,
I visit you in Ashland.

We watch ash trees
drop their orange leaves
and you shampoo my hair.

You make soup of
water from a spring,
carrots and local salt.
It boils all day. We share
a single spoon.

Boughs of ancient ash trees,
I discover when I'm home,
once were carved to spears
used to keep peace.

        Wands of ash were used
        as rods, to heal.

Ash leaves were laid flat
beneath one's pillow
to call in prophetic dreams.

    An ash grove speeds our change.

The tree of life, for druids,

was an ash—its roots
like spirals to the lower world,
its wreath of leaves with God.

I am stretched that way.

My mind is looped in peace,
most days,

my gut and ribcage nestle in black soil,

my toes clasp inner earth.
'

The dream I dream awake
is what's to be. I find I'm mostly tree—

and so are you. We root
to fruit, to see.

DURING MEDITATION

During meditation,
I listen to the sound that's
always ringing—

the high bells of creation.

When I asked my mother
what that sound was—
I'd listen, as a small child,
in my bedroom—she told me
there was nothing.

I begged
she listen with me,
and we listened.

I heard the air was tolling
like a gold bell—

she told me
there was nothing.

Now
I spend my mornings
hearing carefully
all aspects of that pealing

it takes all time to make—

on its low end, buzzing
of a lit world—
a kind of bare wire hanging—
    the electric shock
    that is—

higher, a kind of
holy ringing—

higher,
crystal singing—

       the song that water makes
       in air—

mist that climbs the waterfall's
high cresting—

    and billows colors—

       a mist that alters.

I listen to that sound
and it grows bigger—

     what undergirds us

      becomes a river.

Gonging, dinging, chiming,

and the friction
of all things rubbed together—

it's *this*
that loops the weather—

most days,
it is too quiet to measure—

some days, it's an ether
for the taker—

      its high provides
      forever.

THE HERMIT'S SONG

These months alone,
an oblong cave
of wonders,
crystals forming
rafters,
the bats
black asters.

An ordinary torch
revealed stalactites
dripping into dark pools
that harbored otters.

These months alone,
I spread the book
of order. Dazzled
in my monk's robe.
Ate just
spring water.

I rode
the lazy river, twisting
slowly,
saw the
clotted starlings.
They'd lift
and scatter.

These months alone,
I curled and slept
in grandeur,
cradled in
pure lightning—
a buzzing manger.

I stepped out of the water
opalescent—
colors spread
upon me—
I was their altar.

It's not just that the hermit
has no master—
it's that, far and shuttered,
he's learning faster.

You think he's a cake
that stays a batter.

He's the dark reaction
that builds all matter.

FOR A CERTAIN GROVE OF OAKS
TAKEN BY THE WOOLSEY FIRE

For ten days I've been calm.
Earth inhales her forests and then
breathes them out again as
sprigs and shoots. Nothing
that she does is ever wrong—
even ancient branches as they burn
know that—
whirled as embers, ash, they think
as seed.

I've known ten days
the loss was mine.
Sucked as smoke into the
mother tree,
each leaf I'd loved, each trunk
would swirl in high ecstatic light,

become the bird they'd long admired,
suddenly,
        and too his lift, his flight,

and after much elation, curl,
then sleep in sod,
then speak as one good bud,

and what could be as sweet?
But those were mine, those trunks,

so loved, so climbed,
those braided chairs I spent
round, perfect hours in,
toward sky.

Today I mourn for you,
although you cannot die,

you hoop of oaks
that looped me as I'd heal.

Oh, favorite, with branches
like a ladder
from the barrel of the lower world,

your life helped mine.
    On ash-white ground, I kneel.

GRAY

I wish
there were many words
for gray. We think of ash,
or silt—some matter's end,
or grime that's in between.
Also there is this:
first early morning
under mist,
a clean gray,
and also gray that cleans.

Here there is
the bright light
of all being,
but dimmed and calmed
by particles of water,
a gentle form
of freshening.

Baptism in increments,
the function
of this mist—
this gray of doves
that heals us
quietly,
then lifts.

IN KENYA

I trusted that something
was coming for me.
I heard it say,
Go there and something will come.
One night—I'd been there
a week—I rose
from the fathoms of sleep
into masterful wakefulness—
as if pulled,
as if willed, by calm power—
    and quickly sat up.

A flashlight's beam suddenly
swept down my tent
of taut canvas
on stilts—I was deep
in the bush—

    and
across this graceful scrim
a shadow moved, made by a
towering body,

and I heard one long elephant sigh.

      He breathed from a depth
      that breached earth,
      with a sound

that was pure earth,

        and his flag of an ear
        brushed my tent.

           I felt him as he moved.

Sound of his flowing, high,
monolith weight,

his gianteen sway,

his thick, voluptuous gait—

        I was all awake.

        That perfect shadow of his form—
        assured, anointed,
        rapturous, upright—
           hallowed my plain tent.

Look at him, I heard—
Hungry, he eats.

When he's sleepy, flattens
between trees.

Daily he rejoices,
splashes
with his slim,

cavorting trunk.

    It is
    not work.

Look at the body
I've given to you,
it said.

How is it shaped?

What did you come here
to use it for?

    Be light.

ONE MONARCH BUTTERFLY

Yesterday your city
passed our city,
fluttered down our streets,
looped buildings,
swirled our collared shirts at lunch.

Now I fly from bed
and find your kind has gone,
flown south,
except for you.

     You amble down my street.

This
I must have seemed
hiking at summer camp,
the whole group far downstream.

     And also
     my whole life.

Last monarch,
last King of Air,
flattened, freckled robes as light
as light itself—
are you focused southward,
or—like me—
up?

THE TEAROOM AT CRAIL HARBOUR

Tiny as a studio apartment,
its whole back faced the sea.
I'd sit and drink my tea,
day after day, and eat
one bowl of crisps,

    and watch the light split clouds.

    It was the sort of place
I'd pass while traveling—
an ancient, stone-walled building,

    iron knocker,
    seated on a cliff,

        wavy glass,
        paned windows,

cluttered as a cottage,

like the cliff it sat on,
shaped by sea—

and enter,
and know a glowing hour,
    trying to commit to mind
    the view, the light,
    the smell—

and leave, promising myself
I'd find a month
to come and stay nearby,

and never see again.

To a Californian, unfathomably old,
its walls had stood
perhaps a thousand years.

The window panes had each been blown
from sand to glass
by human air.

Tourists came and went.
Not many, it was winter, it was raining,
but a few did come.

I did not go—

I lived five months nearby.

Finally, I'd turned off the projector
on some tourist's handmade movie

and stepped inside one frame.

Cream in my tea,
crisps in a small white bowl,

sea in black and navy,
wide, alive, unbroken,
sometimes striped with green.

Always, that room stayed as fresh
as waking, as the first thought
in the morning: your eyes still shut,
you think, *What should I build*.

DYING FLOWERS

What luxury
one sees
in dying flowers,
like this group,

the boughs of gladiolus
in an operatic droop,

the lilies shy
and pinking,
their blooms bowed
toward the crowd,

in deference
for clapping,
gone all slack.

Oh,
to have performed well,
as these flowers did,
and know—

to bow low,
and feel high,
having sung.

The violins
still in your ears,

your costume on,
to lean down

and be done.

THE VICTIM EXPERIENCE

A friend told me
he'd paid for the victim experience—
had, with others,
hired several men
to hold his head in water,
drag him by the hair.

    Hundreds paid for this.

Oh, what we'll endure
when love is too good—
or beauty, peace.

Oh, the walls we'll build a while
against love.

      When the portal that our breath can form
      direct to heaven
      is too stark.

      When the bells of quiet
      are too soft.

        When we're sure their peal—
        its blown-glass stairway—
        we don't deserve.

Oh, what we'll endure

when grace
is too much—
too bright. Too sweet.

When we
and our own kindness
are
too much.

EMPLOYEE AT THE ROLLER RINK

Not as old as my father is, but
gray above the ears

is the man in the referee shirt
and black skates
who expertly cuts between us,
forwards then backwards,
at the teeming roller rink.

Hips as his delicate rudder,
slight left and hard right,
he navigates, then spins—
work, celebration, and work.

In the new world, he is saying
with his body, *what we love most
will support us—*
arabesque,
lunge, glide.

Elegant, his footwork,
or inspired, and his thorax
is open and lithe.

He becomes
the music.

It's like
being foam on a wave,
say his arms, which are dancing—

the sea makes you,
and it lifts you,
and you ride.

TO OUTLIVE

You, who are reading,
do you think
I cannot
see you,
slumped inside
your frayed pajamas,
living?

Do you think
I outlived
something easy?
No:
none of us,
not you, not she,
came to earth
to live through
something paltry.

No soul
braves the body,
no soul
leaves the ethers
and the bell's call
and the light's swirl
lightly.

No soul
takes the trip

to outlive nothing.

No one
took to form
that didn't
need it:

didn't need
the learning,

didn't need
the hard
it took
to get it.

I can see you doubt
that it was worth it.

That's what you'll
learn last,
but fast:

      It was.
      And why
      it was.

There will be
a burst of brightness,
feeling.

You will know
that to
outlive
is living.

FLY

Candle, something died
in you—a fly is preserved
on its side
in your light-colored wax,
slim antennae
reaching.

Still facing
the flame.

Still, in some ways,
flying.

I too hover near
your torch
(a scrim, a veil)
as it flickers
this world, other world,
and wonder
how close I can get.

Wings akimbo,
gaze enraptured,
trailing two
eyelash-thin legs.

His shape is Icarus falling,
but up.

HOUSEWORK

Wash,
sweep,

but the rooms
are never tidy
at the same time.
I sit
in the ordered one,
delighting.

I eat
in the ordered one.
I pray.
*Books are in their
handsome stacks,*
I think.

Something always sliding
from the center. Something
centered.
Labor—bending, washing,
then: one room.

POEM FOR MY CAR

Old pal, today
I got the news you passed
your test and can
propel again.

I celebrate
your hundred thousand miles—
wise, I say,
to potholes,
ditches, dirt.

Hills
you cannot mount
as you did once, when you
were sprightlier—

those years,
you and I would spend
the paper money I would make
in offices—
a board game prop—
fluming up the coast.

Dust storms
in the desert
left you
tan and marbled, once—

like fine
Italian paper.

You were brave.

This year, Utah ice
across your windshield
made the glass
high up in churches—

mottled,
swirled, opaque.

I melted it
with tea.

You've been
only mine.
Most years we have had
no passengers.

Spark plugs, cam shaft,
alternator, belts—
        where is the reaction
        that creates your calm
        and guile?

Ribcage, thymus,
larynx, muscle, vein—

my case, too, is wise
to dips and potholes,
and spurred on by flame.

AUTOBIOGRAPHY

I was born with peace
across my sight.

      No education
      could change my shimmered vision,

            or rearrange this fixed
            orientation.

I can see a city
calm and risen,
opalescent,
satin, clockwork,
on the one
we have been given.

Here, said God,
a prism for each eye.

Road oil will show rainbows
in your low
but floating heaven,

and your robe
will be of concrete.

      Now
      try to leven.

Many years I've lived this way—
    how have I managed?

A stranger might say,
Strangely.

The poignant thing:
I've lived.

I lean into precision,
not perfection.

    Letting what I *can* do
    be enough for me—

    that softness—

is my

    lesson.

THE WATER IN THE VASE

For a day, I could not
find the odor—
putrid, stinging,
with the distressing affect
of a sharp clarinet.

It was the flowers' water.
I had not thought to look there.

Beneath where they had bloomed,
and sagged—a sewer.

The distance they had launched us,
each graceful bud, bright leaf—

a spike in the graph of pleasure—
straight up—one sweet cliff—

was the very distance that smell
plunged us,
rotting, irksome,

wondering what in our home
had gone so foul.

Like the thoughts this morning
of a former love I can't believe I harbored,

left with its water.

That's how loves are managed—
we stand on beauty's cliff-edge—

looped by bracing sea air—
alert—and most alive—

later, the ground's a far-off ceiling
we stare at with a longing:
        a holy arch.

One can build a good hut
on the meadow—
a steady hut.
A hut made for hard weather.
I have not.

Pouring out the water
from the tall vase,
I breathe in all its rancor.

        I honor it,
and bloom.

LILIES

I'm sweeping up
the lilies' fragrant stamens,

which drop flurries of red dust—

a mess
that many times
has stained a chair or shirt.

Carefully, like trying
to corral a bird,
I broom them to the dustpan,
move it gingerly;
still, my hands are blotched.

Once again I bought
six fragrant lilies
at the farmer's market,
put them in a jar
and let them spread.

So far they have birthmarked
one gray sweater,
the pants I love to sleep in,
my bedspread, one pillow
and one sock.

They are like the friends,

ten years ago,
who turned up what was playing
on the radio
and danced atop my car.

    Necklaces and boots
    and skirts and long hair
    flew above the afternoon
    in wide, ecstatic arcs.

Later, my mechanic
sagged his shoulders
when he saw the dents and scratches
on my car's roof,

    which I would not fix.

Ten years. Those old breezy friends—
one moved east with troubles,
two I hardly see—
dance above me still.

All this week, the heavy scent
these lilies flumed
made affluent and lucky
this one corner of my life.

Here each widened bloom
channeled pure jungle—
marked each afternoon

as flourishing, as lush,
as sweet, alive.

The red
can stay.

WRITING

I stop meditating, start a poem—
step from one light haze, enter another,
all creation swirling, pausing, forming,
and I chose to heed: I feel its meaning,
feel its need to be and stand up quickly,
stagger to my desk, full of a something
not completely known, but brimming, crowning,
and midwife that body into being.
Does the baby choose its mother, growing?
Did the mother choose the child she's holding?
Are we paired like partners for group dancing?
Fresh, and with a will I can feel coming,
into my own arms arrives this something.

TINY HOUSES

This year, we are
building
smaller houses,

sleeping
in compartments,

hammering
comportment.

Small,
we say, we build,

to mean
efficient,

to need less
from the system,

our girth
to bravely
lessen.

We are brave
to live
outside of heaven—

that's our great
concession—

not to live
efficiently:
to live.

Already
there's
concision.

That's
our sole
decision.

Not to live without
our many
mansions,

but to
plain forget
that we are in them.

FLY IN WATER

I can't blame you, housefly
that is drowning
in the lilies' water.

    My nose is deep in them,
and they have not yet bloomed.

Patience
is a monk's easy genius;
next week I will learn it.
    Next week I will sit.

Now my nose is wedged
into the corridor
that happily will spread
into a kingdom, if I step aside
and wait.

Time
is a monk's bright luxury—
it's his glowing robe.
    Not mine.
I nose, I stare,
I nose.

SIXTEEN STATEMENTS ABOUT EMPTY ROOMS

It feels good to give our things away.
Friends won't want your empty rooms to stay.
Keeping one's rooms empty takes sharp will.
What is empty calculates to fill.

Ownership exacts a kind of rent.
Clutter is a tenant that can't pay.
When we do not own, we will invent.
It feels good to give our things away.

Emptiness can also mark a place.
What is born is born in open space.
Every color's waiting in clear light.
Plain walls cause a rainbowing of sight.

Monks fill empty rooms with quiet prayer.
Nothing there, you see what's always there.
Seeing nothing is what builds your sight.
Prisms will emerge in rooms of white.

HOLY FLIGHT

I wait for it,
and now and then, it comes: I dream
I'm on a balcony

    and know that I can jump.

          Oh,
           holy flight—

straight down, and fast,
    my long hair flapping,

    grinning,

softened limbs, no gripping—

one long fall while held.

        Sweet, the whole descent—
        lighter than childhood—

better than a creaking built amusement,
as heaven cannot break.

    To jump and fall and know
    there's only flight—

        a warm exhilaration

we can't quite know here.

I am good at
sleeping while aware.

    Nothing to malfunction,
nothing to endure
when the body lands,
    I climb the banister.

Rapture, speed,
soft air—

the sound of my
ecstatic hair—

and power:

both arrowhead
and archer,

      both here, awake,
      and there.